D0099497

The
First Christmas Tree

To ALL who seek to worship God
in spirit and in truth.
(John 3:23, 24)

And to Paul and Jonathan
Two gifted members of our family,
Who lead many young people in worship
And whose hearts are very much like the Littlest Fir Tree.

THANKS!
With heartfelt appreciation to Jeannie Taylor,
And to Barbara Martin and Connie Soth
For encouragement and for excellence in editing.

Text ©1997 Helen Haidle
Illustrations © 1997 David Haidle

Published by New Kids Media™ in association with Baker Book House Company, P.O.
Box 6287, Grand Rapids, Michigan 49516-6287.

All rights reserved. No part of this publication may be reproduced, stored in a retrieval
system, or transmitted in any form or by any means whatsoever—electronic, mechanical,
photocopy, recording, or any other—without the prior written permission of the publisher.
The only exception is brief quotations in printed reviews.

ISBN—0-8010-4393-X

Published and
distributed in
association with

The
First Christmas Tree

Helen Haidle

Illustrated by

David Haidle
&
Elizabeth Haidle

$\mathcal{L}$ong ago, it has been told, a tiny green shoot broke
through the blanket of pine needles in a shady woodland.

"At last!" said the new little fir, stretching upward.

The grandfather fir tree smiled down in surprise and
said kindly, "Hi there, little fellow."

Other towering forest trees ignored the littlest fir
as he bent this way and that, straining to catch
some sunshine.

Many seasons passed. The straggly little tree
waited patiently, hoping to grow strong and
majestic like the trees he admired.

*T*hen one day, an eagle swooped through the highest treetops and cried in a shrill voice, "The Promised One is coming soon! Prepare to celebrate His birth!"

The announcement echoed among the woodlands, stirring up great excitement among the animals and birds.

The trees rustled their branches with anticipation.

A tall pine tree announced, "I'll bring Him a gift of my large pine cones."

"I'll give my finest apples," said the old apple tree.

"My branches will make beautiful wreaths," said the fir.

W hy is everyone so excited? What is happening?"
the little fir asked the squirrels and rabbits scurrying past
him. No one answered. They were too busy.

"Prepare our best!" the animals called to each other as
they scampered throughout the forest and orchard.

"Search for the biggest walnuts, acorns, and seeds!"

"Bring wild berries and grain to our storage place."

"Gather only the *finest* for our King's Son."

*I*n the midst of the hurry-scurry, a furry-tailed bundle fell through the air, landing with a thud near the little tree.

"Help!" whimpered the baby squirrel, but the other animals hurried past, busy with their preparations.

"I'll help you," called the kindhearted little tree. "Try to climb onto my branch. But be quick. Danger is near."

The little tree lowered a branch
to the baby squirrel who hobbled onto it.
   "Shhh," whispered the littlest fir tree as a fox
bounded down the path in search of food.
"Hide in my branches. You can stay as
long as you like." He hummed a
lullaby, swayed in the breeze,
and rocked the baby
squirrel to sleep.

When the baby squirrel woke up later, the littlest fir tree asked, "Will *you* tell me who is coming?"

"Oh, yes! My Daddy told me that the King's Son is going to be born. He's coming from Heaven as a human baby."

"Why is *He* coming?" asked the littlest fir.

"To fix everything that is wrong on earth. He will bring us love and new life. My family will give Him our finest nuts."

*T*hat night the little tree was unable to sleep.
His heart leaped for joy as he thought, *The Son of the
King is coming! Is He the One who scattered the stars and
painted the sunset? What gift can I give Him?*

*T*he next morning, the little tree asked the cardinal, "What are *you* giving the King's Son?"

"When the dear Child is born," said the bird. "I will pluck the finest feather from my wing as a gift for Him."

I wish I had something beautiful like a red feather, thought the little tree, feeling worried. *I don't know what to give.*

Cooler breezes blew through the forest when the eagle's message finally rang out: "The Promised Child has come at last. Bring your gifts to His place of birth!"

The woodland creatures and trees selected the finest of all they had gathered. Carrying their gifts, they began the happy procession to the town at the bottom of the hill.

$\mathcal{T}$he little tree felt a ripple of excitement from the tip of his tallest branch down to his roots. He moved forward to join the procession.

"WAIT!" ordered the apple tree. "Where are *you* going?"

"To . . . to see the King's Son," he said.

The apple tree scowled. "Your branches are empty."

A stately oak, laden with acorns, laughed at the little tree. "Don't embarrass us by coming. You don't have a gift."

The littlest fir sadly moved aside, hoping no one would notice him. He watched the birds fly towards town and the woodland creatures descend the hill carrying pine cones, grain, fruit, nuts, berries, and dripping honeycombs.

They're right, he thought. *I am not worthy to go. I have nothing to give.*

While the sad little fir watched everyone leave, a whimpering sound interrupted his thoughts. He looked down and saw two little shivering mice.

"What's wrong?" he asked them.

"We were taking gifts to the Newborn," they said, "but now we've lost our mother."

He gently wrapped his branch around them. "Snuggle next to my trunk, little ones. I'll help you find her."

$\mathcal{P}$art way down the hill, the littlest tree
saw a bluebird fluttering above the path.

"Watch out for my egg!" she cried. "My nest slipped off
the branch of the giant pine. Please don't trample my egg!"

"Don't worry. I'll keep you and your egg safe," said the
little tree, gently edging a branch under the nest.

$\mathcal{R}$elieved, the bluebird settled onto her nest while the littlest fir slowly descended the hill, carefully balancing his branches. He couldn't help worrying about what the other trees might say when they saw him.

$\mathcal{A}$t the bottom of the hill, the woodland
creatures were crowded around the entrance of a stable.
The mother bird whispered, "You're the last one
here because you stopped to help me. I'm sorry."
"I don't mind," said the littlest fir in a low voice.
"I have nothing to give. I just came to help the lost mice."
He tried to move closer, but the trees scowled
and blocked him with their branches.
"Why did you come?" they asked.
"You don't have a gift!"

*I*t's no use, thought the little tree. *I'll never get close enough to see the newborn Child. But I'm so glad He's here.*

The littlest fir closed his eyes and reverently bowed his branches.

Overhead, God the King was watching.

An angel called out, "Stars of heaven! Come down and light up the branches of the littlest fir tree!"

A swirl of glittering stars cascaded downward, filling the branches of the little tree. The bright glow spread — from a star on top, to sparkles on every branch.

"Oh, LOOK!" cried the two young mice.
The littlest fir opened his eyes. *What is shining?*
he wondered. Looking around, he discovered
the stars on all his branches. "It's *me*!" he cried.
"*I'm* the one who's shining!"

Everyone turned to see where
the bright light was coming from.
They stared at the glittering
tree, then slowly moved
back, opening a path
to the stable.

The littlest fir gazed upon the
child at last. "I'm . . . I'm so glad you came,"
stammered the littlest fir. "I wish I had something to give you."

The Baby smiled at him. Then an angel spoke from above:
"God accepts your thanks and praise — they are the best
gifts of all. When you helped others, you did what God's Son
has come to do. Now go. Continue to serve Him in love."

The woodland trees honored the littlest fir with an open space at the top of the hill.

He became a favorite nesting place for small animals and birds. They always asked to hear the story of when the little tree wore stars at the birth of the King's Son.

And each year, when they celebrated the Child's birthday, glittering stars of heaven came down once again to light up . . . the very first *Christmas tree*.

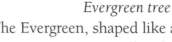

The Meaning of
Christmas Decorations

Evergreen tree
The Evergreen, shaped like an arrowhead,
points to Heaven. Its needles always remain green,
reminding us of God's gift of eternal LIFE,
and of Jesus' living presence in our homes.
(1 John 5:11-12)

Stars
Stars on the tree remind us
of the star of Bethlehem *(Matthew 2:1-10)*.

Angels
God's angels announced Jesus' birth:
to Mary, to Joseph, and to the shepherds *(Luke 1 & 2)*.

Lights & Candles
Jesus called Himself the "Light of the world" *(John 9:5)*,
and also called *us* lights of the world *(Matthew 4:14)*.

Red decorations
Red is a color that symbolizes LOVE.
God loved the world and sent Jesus to be our Savior.
Because Jesus loved us,
He gave His life for us on the cross.
(Mark 8:31)

Gold decorations
Jesus is the KING of kings *(Revelation 1:5)*.

Gifts under tree
Gifts remind us of God's greatest gift — Jesus,
and of the gifts of the Wise Men.
(John 3:16, Matthew 2:1-12)

IDEAS
for
PARENTS:

When you decorate your Christmas tree, read this legend of the first of many trees decorated in remembrance of God's greatest Gift — Jesus.

Christmas trees remind us of the living presence of Jesus in our homes. Jesus promised, *"Surely I will be with you always, to the very end of the age."* (Matthew 28:20) and *"Where two or three come together in my name, there am I with them."* (Matthew 18:20)

Discussion & Activities

♦ Before Christmas, take time to sit by the lights of your Christmas tree, eat tree-shaped cookies, and read parts of Luke chapter 1. Read about Mary and Martha (Luke 10:38-42). What pleased Jesus? Why? How do we "sit at Jesus' feet"? Let everyone share something for which they are thankful.

♦ Talk about preparing our hearts, as well as our homes, for the celebration of Jesus' birth. Share ideas of how to spend time with God, and how to make *Jesus* the focus of all Christmas celebrations. Set aside time from baking, shopping, etc., and give Jesus a gift of love and worship from your heart. Should any activities be eliminated to make more time for God and for others? *(Remember the woodland creatures who didn't have "time" to help?)*

♦ Buy or make a manger scene with nonbreakable figures that children can use to retell the Christmas story. Fill a *dress-up box* with shawls, robes, head coverings, and cloth remnants. Let children act out events in the first two chapters of Matthew and Luke in the Bible. Invite neighbors and relatives to see the play. Serve Christmas tree cookies and read this book.

♦ Share a quiet time by candlelight. Read God's Word *(Psalms 135-150 are excellent praise psalms)*. Meditate on Scriptures of Jesus' birth *(Matthew 1-2 and Luke 1-2)*. Pray silently or together, give thanks, worship, kneel by your beds, etc.

♦ Sing together familiar songs of praise and worship. Help children focus on Jesus and what He has done. Encourage them to make up their own songs or put new words to familiar tunes.

Prepare a Manger-Bed for Jesus

We serve Jesus when we serve others. Jesus said: *"Whatever you did for one of the least of these brothers of mine, you did for me."* (Matthew 25:40)

1. Place a basket or shoebox *(Jesus' manger-bed)* under your Christmas tree.
2. Fill another box with straw and place it nearby.
    When anyone is a helper, does a kind deed, or encourages someone else, they can put one straw into the manger-bed.
3. On Christmas Eve, place a baby doll on top of the bed of hay.
    Talk about how everyone helped prepare the *"bed"* for Jesus.

OR: Ask your children what they would give Baby Jesus if He were born at your house today. During the weeks before Christmas, let them place in the "manger" the gifts *they* consider to be important. Pray together about where to take the gifts, as you GIVE to Jesus by giving to others.

Scroll Gifts for Jesus

Whatever we do for others is a gift for Jesus (Matthew 25:40).
- Cut Christmas wrapping paper into small rectangles (about 4" x 4").
- Write down some act of kindness you will do for someone else.
- Roll up rectangle like a scroll, tie with ribbon, place on tree branch.

Giving in Secret

Read Matthew 6:1-4 and pray about giving *secret* gifts to family or friends, or adopting a needy family. "Giving Trees" also provide opportunities to give without receiving thanks. Pray for those who receive the gifts.